¡Hola, ¡Lola!

Guatemalan Summer

BY KEKA NOVALES

ILLUSTRATED BY GLORIA FÉLIX

PICTURE WINDOW BOOKS
a capstone imprint

Published by Picture Window Books, an imprint of Capstone.
1710 Roe Crest Drive, North Mankato, Minnesota 56003
capstonepub.com

Library of Congress Cataloging-in-Publication Data
Names: Novales, Keka, author. | Félix, Gloria, illustrator.
Title: Guatemalan summer / by Keka Novales ; illustrated by Gloria Felix.
Description: North Mankato, Minnesota : Picture Window Books, an
imprint of Capstone, [2023] | Series: ¡Hola, Lola! | Audience: Ages 5–7.
| Audience: Grades K–1. | Text primarily in English; some words in
Spanish. | Summary: Lola is excited to go to Guatemala with Abuelita for
a few weeks to learn about her heritage and see her family, but when she
arrives, things do not go as planned. Her Spanish is not as good as she
thought, and she feels out of place.
Identifiers: LCCN 2021047087 (print) | LCCN 2021047088 (ebook) |
ISBN 9781666337266 (hardcover) | ISBN 9781666343892 (paperback) |
ISBN 9781666343939 (pdf)
Subjects: LCSH: Grandmothers—Juvenile fiction. | Families—
Guatemala—Juvenile fiction. | Guatemalans--Social life and customs—
Juvenile fiction. | Guatemala—Juvenile fiction. | Guatemala—Fiction.
| CYAC: Grandmothers—Fiction. | Family life—Guatemala—Fiction. |
Guatemalans—Social life and customs—Fiction. | LCGFT: Novels.
Classification: LCC PZ7.1.N683 Gu 2023 (print) | LCC PZ7.1.N683
(ebook) | DDC [Fic]—dc23
LC record available at https://lccn.loc.gov/2021047087
LC ebook record available at https://lccn.loc.gov/2021047088

Design Elements: Shutterstock/g_tech, Shutterstock/Olgastocker

Designed by Kay Fraser

TABLE OF CONTENTS

Meet Lola!

¡Hola, I'm Lola! I live in Texas with my family—Mama, Dad, and my baby sister, Mariana. The rest of my family, including my grandparents, live in Guatemala. That's where my parents are from. I know lots of interesting facts about the country.

Facts About Guatemala

- Guatemala is in Central America. It is about the size of the state of Tennessee.
- Guatemala has 37 volcanoes, but only three are active—that means they're erupting. The other 34 are asleep.
- The official language in Guatemala is Spanish.

Facts About Me

- I'm learning Spanish.
- I love history. I want to be an archaeologist when I grow up.
- I adore my family.
- I don't like change.
- I hate Mondays and onions, not to mention waking up early. Yuck!

My Family

Mama likes to speak Spanish at home. She is always trying to teach me about my roots and culture. Here are some other facts about Mama:

- She loves chocolate.
- She misses her family in Guatemala and wishes we saw them more often.
- She hates clutter!

Dad travels a lot for work. Since he is gone so much, our family time is extra special. Here are some other facts about Dad:

- He loves cars.
- He hates being late.
- He always makes us laugh!

Abuelita, my grandma, is one of my favorite people. She visits us once or twice a year. It is magical when we are together. She has the best stories. Here are some other facts about Abuelita:

- She cooks the best food and gives the best advice.
- She knows how to do just about anything.
- She is my favorite!

Abuelo, my grandpa, spends most of his time in Guatemala. (Don't tell anyone, but I think he is afraid of planes!) Here are some other facts about Abuelo:

- He loves Abuelita's cooking!
- He is always happy.
- He loves singing, telling jokes, and being playful.

Chapter 1

Going to Guatemala!

Mama woke me up *early* Sunday morning. It was so early that I thought I was dreaming.

"Five more minutes," I said as I rolled over. I am *not* a morning person.

"You don't want to be late!" Mama replied.

I opened my eyes and saw a giant suitcase perfectly packed. Then I remembered—I was going to Guatemala!

That was where Abuelita lived. My grandmother stayed with us for a few months every year, but it was time for her to go home.

My parents thought it would be fun for me to tag along. It would give me a chance to practice my Spanish. Plus, Abuelita wanted me to understand my heritage and roots.

I was mainly excited to spend time with my cousins! We talked to them on the phone sometimes, but I hadn't seen most of them since I was a baby. I was extra excited to see my cousin Luis. He was my age.

Still . . . I was a little nervous about going to another country for two weeks. It was my first time traveling without my parents.

Abuelita was waiting for me downstairs. "¡Hola, Lola!" she greeted me.

"Morning, Abuelita," I replied.

"Ready to go to Guatemala?" she asked.

I nodded excitedly. "I can't wait!"

Mama double-checked that we had my ticket and passport before we left the house. I would need it to enter Guatemala and come back to the United States.

"What do you have in here, Lola? Did you pack rocks?" Dad asked.

Dad pretended to struggle as he loaded our luggage into the car. I giggled. My suitcase was so full that it looked like I was moving to Guatemala instead of just visiting.

At the airport, it was time to say our goodbyes. Abuelita gave Mama and Dad hugs and kisses. Then it was my turn.

Dad squeezed me tightly. "Bye, Lola!"

I blew kisses to Mariana. My baby sister was fast asleep in her car seat.

"Have fun! I'll call you tonight," Mama said as she hugged me.

I put on my backpack and rolled my suitcase into the airport. We waited at the gate to board.

"Why don't you take the window seat?" Abuelita suggested when we got to our row on the plane. "I want you to see the mountains and volcanoes when we fly into Guatemala."

"Yes, please!" I replied.

The plane took off, and Abuelita and I talked about all the things I wanted to do in Guatemala. I was dying to see the famous volcanoes! My parents had told me all about them.

Eventually, Abuelita fell asleep. I tried to sleep too, but I was too excited to close my eyes.

Then it was time to get a snack and a drink. The flight attendant gave me a cup of juice. I munched on some pretzels as I stared out the window at the ocean. After a while, I saw mountains too!

Abuelita woke up as we were getting ready to land. When the plane touched down, people started to clap.

"Abuelita, why are they clapping?" I asked.

"La Aurora is one of the most dangerous airports in the world," Abuelita explained. "People like to clap after a safe landing."

I started to clap and cheer too. Now that we were safely on the ground, I was ready to start exploring Guatemala!

Chapter 2

Welcome

Abuelita and I stepped off the plane. Together, we made our way through the airport.

Outside, the air smelled different. There was a sweet smell of flowers, coffee, and something else.

While waiting, I noticed all the signs were in Spanish. It felt so different from home.

When we walked out the exit, Abuelo and my uncle Hector were waiting.

"¡Hola, Lola!" Abuelo said. He gave me a bear hug. "I've missed you so much. How was your flight?"

But before I could answer, my uncle interrupted.

"Look at you! You are so big! I'm Tío Hector, your favorite uncle!" he said. "Just call me Tío."

His words made me feel out of place. I knew who Tío Hector was. He was Mama's brother. We talked on the phone for birthdays and special occasions.

Why is he acting like we don't know each other? I wondered. *Am I different in person?*

"¡Vámonos!" Tío hollered. He led the way to his blue minivan.

As we exited the airport, Tío pointed to a big clock made of flowers. "That's el Reloj de Flores," he explained. "The numbers on there are Mayan numerals."

Abuelita and my parents always told me stories about the Mayans. That was part of why I wanted to be an archaeologist when I grew up.

The ride to Abuelita's house was slow. There were cars and colorful buses around us.

We finally made it to my grandparents' house. It was a one-story home with a beautiful garden in the front.

We went in through the kitchen. There was a woman inside waiting for us.

"¡Buenas tardes!" she said.

"Lola, let me introduce you to Oralia. She is our housekeeper. She has been with our family since your Mama was a baby!" said Abuelita.

I had never been to a home with a housekeeper before. I smiled at Oralia.

"¡Hola!" I said.

"Oralia made tamales for dinner. And your favorite, chocolate caliente," Abuelita told me. "I'll let you in on the secret ingredient. It's amor—love."

"Gracias," I said to Oralia. I loved chocolate caliente. It was one of Abuelita's best recipes. I always felt special when she made it for me.

Abuelita showed me into the living room. My eyes widened with surprise. It seemed like a hundred people were waiting for us!

Everyone started waving, smiling, hugging, and kissing me all at once. I had never seen so many aunts, uncles, cousins, and neighbors.

A girl with green eyes and dark hair came up to me. "Hi! I'm Isabel!" she said. "I'm your abuelita's neighbor."

"Hi," I replied. "I'm Lola."

Tío came up to me with his wife, Tía Luz, and their kids, Luis and Dieguito. Dieguito was only two years old, but Luis was my age.

"Luis, you remember your cousin Lola!" Tío said. "You two are going to be great friends!"

"Hi!" I said with a smile.

"¡Hola!" Luis said.

He leaned forward like he was going to kiss me on the cheek. I stepped back quickly.

I knew greeting people with a kiss on the cheek was normal in Guatemala, but I wasn't used to it. I gave him a little wave instead.

Luis frowned. He seemed confused, but he waved back.

Just then, the phone rang. Abuelita came and gave it to me. It was Mama. I took the phone into the other room.

"¡Hola, Lola! How was your flight?" Mama asked.

"Good," I said. "But there are *a lot* of people here at Abuelita's house."

Mama chuckled. "Enjoy getting to know everyone," she said. "I'm so happy you have this chance to see where I grew up and learn about where we're from."

"Me too. I just miss Texas. Everything here is so different. Love you!" I said.

After talking with Mama, I felt a little homesick.

I wish my family was in Guatemala with me, I thought.

But I knew Mama wanted me to have fun. I went back to the party and found Isabel.

"Do you want to play outside?" I asked.

"Sure!" Isabel agreed.

Luis joined us, and we went to the trampoline in the yard.

"I have the same trampoline at home," I said. "Only ours is bigger."

"Cool!" Isabel replied.

Luis bounced and did a flip. "Can you do flips?" he asked me.

"Yup!" I did two in a row.

"Show-off!" Luis exclaimed.

I frowned. I hadn't meant to show off.
Before I could say that, Tío called us inside.

"Niños, a comer," he said. "Children, time
to eat."

I followed my cousin and Isabel inside.
I didn't think I'd given Luis a very good first
impression. I had to show him who I truly was.

Chapter 3

Homesick

I sat with Luis and Isabel at a table in the kitchen. I took a small bite of tamale. It tasted different than when Abuelita made them for me back in Texas. Thinking about that made me feel even more homesick.

Maybe if I tell Luis more about where I'm from, he'll like me better, I thought.

"This is yummy!" I said as I took a bite. "You know what else is yummy? Brisket!"

"What's brisket?" asked Isabel.

"It's the best beef in the world!" I replied. "It's my favorite food back home. My dad smokes it for hours. You would love it."

"There's nothing like Guatemalan food," Luis said.

I smiled. "I'm excited for you to show me around Guatemala!" I said.

"Guate," Luis corrected me.

"Guate?" I asked.

"We don't usually say Guatemala. We say Guate," Isabel explained.

Luis frowned at me. "Everyone knows that."

After dinner, I was tired, even though it wasn't that late. I went back into the living room. The family party was still going.

"Abuelita, I think I'm ready to go to bed," I said with a yawn.

Abuelita nodded. "Traveling can be tiring."

I said goodnight to everyone.

Abuelita took me to my room. It smelled weird, like a mixture of old and some type of cleaner. There were knickknacks everywhere.

"If you need anything, I'll be in the living room until everyone goes home." Abuelita smiled. "¡Buenas noches, Lola!"

"¡Buenas noches, Abuelita!" I replied.

"¡Muy bien, Lola! Your Spanish is getting better!" Abuelita said.

I frowned. My Spanish had seemed okay back in Texas. Abuelita left the room before I could say anything.

I lay in bed for a while, trying to sleep. But I could still hear everyone in the living room. Plus, I was thirsty.

I tiptoed out of my room. I could hear Luis's voice coming from the kitchen.

"She's rude," he was saying. "She didn't give me a kiss when I said hi. And she was acting like a big show-off on the trampoline. Lola thinks she's better than everyone else!"

Me? Better than everyone else? I thought. *What?*

I couldn't see who Luis was talking to. I ran back to my room before they could see me.

I had been so excited to come to Guatemala. But now that I was here, I felt like I didn't belong. Everything felt unfamiliar. I was homesick. I missed my parents and little sister.

My family was from Guatemala, but it didn't feel like I was.

Chapter 4

Antigua

The next morning, a loud sound outside my window woke me up. It sounded like firecrackers! I jumped out of bed and went to find my grandparents. Abuelo and Abuelita were already in the dining room.

"¡Hola, Abuelo!" I said. "¡Hola, Abuelita!"

"¡Buenos días, Lola!" Abuelo said.

"What was that loud noise?" I asked.

"Firecrackers," Abuelita explained. "People set them off all the time here. For birthdays, anniversaries, to get rid of bad spirits."

Guate sure is different from Texas, I thought.

The table in front of me was covered with plates of food. I looked around, hoping for something familiar. Instead, I saw some fruits

I had never seen before, different types of bread, handmade tortillas, and a cheese covered in a green leaf.

"Do you have any pancakes or cereal?" I asked.

Luis came in just then. He scowled at me but gave Abuelo and Abuelita kisses.

"Of course, Lola!" Abuelita said. "We just wanted you to have a taste of Guatemala!"

Luis shook his head. "What else do you want, your majesty?" he whispered.

Tío came over for a cafecito—his morning coffee. I stared at him, thinking about what I'd heard Luis say last night. Did Tío think I was rude too?

"¿No me vas a saludar? Are you going to say hi?" Tío asked with a smile.

"Hi," I said quietly.

Luis rolled his eyes. "Hola," he corrected me. "And you're supposed to give a kiss!"

I kissed Tío on the cheek. I didn't want to seem rude.

"We have a surprise for you today, Lola," Abuelita told me. "We are all going to Antigua! It is a short day trip."

"Antigua!" I cheered.

Mama had told me all about the old city a few hours away. It was surrounded by mountains and volcanoes!

"We're going to have lunch and do some exploring," Abuelita said. "There are lots of colorful buildings and churches."

I grinned. I couldn't wait to see Guate!

In the car, Dieguito gave me a book to read. It was in Spanish.

I've got this, I thought as I read.

"La casa," I said. "Look at the house, Dieguito."

I turned the page. "El pe-r-r-r-ro." I stumbled over my r's.

"Perro," Luis said, rolling his r's easily. "It's not that hard!"

"It is for me!" I exclaimed. "We don't always speak Spanish back home. And all my friends speak English."

"Luis, don't tease your cousin!" said Tía Luz.

Luis grunted.

After two hours, we finally made it to Antigua. The cobblestone streets made for a bumpy ride. Every house had a beautiful metal balcony with an antique door.

"Do they have any shows here?" I asked. "I love going to the Fort Worth Stockyards back home. They have cowboy shows and a longhorn cattle drive!"

Luis frowned. "No shows here," he muttered.

"Look, Lola!" Tío pointed to a perfect crater. "El volcán de Agua," he said.

We parked and went to a hotel. There were flowers everywhere. A band played in the lobby.

"Dance with me, Lola," Abuelo said.

He grabbed my hand and twirled me around the lobby. I giggled.

Abuelita led the way to the hotel restaurant. We got a table on the patio next to a fountain.

"I hope you're not going to ask for cereal again," Luis whispered.

"No, I'll get chicken nuggets!" I joked.

Luis crossed his arms and looked away.

After lunch, we went for a walk. First, we stopped at a candy shop. I spotted something familiar in the window.

"Can we get canillitas de leche? They are my favorite!" I smiled.

"Yum! I want some too," Abuelo replied.

We went to the market. There were so many amazing things. I wanted to buy everything!

I spotted a pair of beautiful silver earrings. They were shaped like roses.

Those would be the perfect gift, I thought.

I turned to Abuelita. "Can I buy those earrings?" I asked. "For Mama."

Abuelita smiled and gave me some colorful money. "Try to practice your Spanish. Here are a hundred quetzales. That's about thirteen dollars," she said.

I looked at the money in my hand. I stared at the earrings. I loved my mama, but what if I got nervous and couldn't say my r's? After what had happened in the car, I worried Luis would make fun of me.

"¡Tú puedes, Lola!" Abuelo cheered me on.

"Don't be afraid! Try your best. If you need me, I'm right here to help you," Abuelita encouraged me.

I turned to the woman selling the earrings. "¿Cuánto?" I asked. "How much?"

"¿Qué se le ofrece?" the lady replied.

I pointed to the rose earrings.

"¿Estos?" She pointed to the wrong pair of earrings.

I could feel my family—including Luis—watching.

"No, la r-r-rosas." I was so nervous that I couldn't roll my r's correctly.

"Las rosas," Luis said to the lady. The words came out easily for him.

"¿Estos?" the lady replied. This time she pointed to the right pair.

I nodded. Why couldn't I roll my r's? Spanish had never seemed like a problem back home.

"Son cien quetzales," the woman told me.

I paid, and she handed me the earrings in a small paper bag.

"Bravo, Lola!" Abuelita cheered. "Speaking another language is hard, but you did it! The more you do it, the more natural it will feel."

But as we moved away, Luis snuck up behind me. "R-r-r-rosas," he whispered. "I thought you knew Spanish."

I blushed and wanted to disappear. I hoped Abuelita was right. Maybe I just needed more practice.

Chapter 5

R's Are Evil

The next morning, Abuelita had something special planned for me.

"You are going to spend the day with Tío's family. It will be a perfect opportunity for you and Luis to bond!" she exclaimed.

NOOOOOO! I thought. Luis and I had not gotten off to a good start.

But maybe Abuelita was right. Maybe this was my chance to be friends with Luis. I could turn things around. I just hoped he would stop giving me such a hard time about my Spanish.

"¡Buenos días, Lola!" Tía Luz greeted me when Abuelito dropped me off.

"Hi!" I replied. This time I remembered to kiss her cheek.

Luis didn't seem impressed. "¡Hola!" he corrected me.

I blushed. Luis was right. I needed to remember to speak Spanish.

"¡Hola!" I said when Tío entered the room.

"¡Hola, Lola!" Tío replied. "You're in for a treat today. We're going to the Popol Vuh Museum! It has one of the largest collections of Mayan art in the world!"

"I can't wait!" I cheered. Then I caught a glimpse of Luis's mad face. "G-rrr-acias."

"¡Gracias!" Luis exclaimed. "Seriously!"

I couldn't roll my r's correctly with Luis around. Those evil r's got stuck on the roof of my mouth like peanut butter!

"Luis, be nice!" Tía Luz scolded.

We drove to the museum. It was at a university. The campus had a lot of brick buildings surrounded by huge trees.

"Cool!" I said, looking around. "This reminds me of my neighborhood back home."

Luis rolled his eyes. He was as good at rolling his eyes as he was at rolling his r's.

We went inside the museum. There were amazing works of art everywhere.

"Look, Luz!" Tío pointed to a sculpture. He and Tía walked over to look at it.

"At home—" I said.

But Luis interrupted. "Can't you enjoy Guate for a second?"

"I didn't mean—" I started.

"I don't know why everyone was so excited for you to come visit," Luis continued. "You're

always bragging about how amazing your home is! You don't even speak Spanish. Are you even Guatemalan?"

He stomped off to the next exhibit to join his parents.

I stared after my cousin and thought about our few days together. Was Luis right?

Maybe I had been talking about home a lot. I missed it and my family. And I'd wanted to share my life there with my cousin. But it was annoying Luis. And I didn't know how to fix things with him.

Chapter 6

You Belong

After the museum, we went back to Tío's house. Tía made tostadas for dinner. They smelled delicious.

"I guess these are all mine," Luis said under his breath. "They're probably not as good as the food you have back home."

I frowned. My parents had always taught me to be proud of my Guatemalan heritage. But now that I was *in* Guatemala, everything was different.

I wanted to fit in. But how? Luis didn't like me. My Spanish was not as good as I'd thought. I was confused.

After dinner, Abuelita came to get me. We walked home. "How was your day?" she asked.

I didn't want to tell her what Luis had said. "Fine," I replied. I put my head down.

"What's the matter, Lola?" Abuelita asked.

I sighed. "Nothing."

Abuelita frowned. "You know you can tell me anything," she said.

I stood quietly for a few seconds.

"I love being with you, Abuelita," I replied. "But I feel like I don't belong here. Everything is different. Everyone corrects me when I speak

Spanish. It's like I'm from another planet!
I miss home."

Abuelita gave me a hug. "It is hard being
away from home," she agreed. "And it can
be hard to find where you belong. Be patient.
Being in Guatemala is an opportunity to learn
new things. Just because things are different
doesn't mean you can't enjoy them."

I nodded. Abuelita always gave good
advice. I had to stop comparing things and
enjoy my time in Guatemala.

* * *

In the morning, Abuelo and I went to the
garden.

"Roses are my favorite flower!" he said.

"Mine too!" I said with a smile.

"What color do you like best? I like the pink
ones!" Abuelo said.

"R-r-rojas. Red" I replied. I covered my face
with my hands. I was embarrassed.

Abuelo hugged me. "Don't feel bad, Lola. Can I tell you a secret? I had a hard time rolling my r's when I was your age."

"Really? I'm not the only one?" I asked.

Abuelo chuckled. "Of course not! R's can be tricky! I practiced day and night until one day, I got them! Don't give up. Keep trying, and eventually they will roll without you thinking about them!"

"I can do this," I said with a smile.

"Yes, you can!" Abuelo replied.

Chapter 7

Tongue Twister

The next day, I had an idea. Maybe Isabel could help me with my Spanish. I hadn't seen her since my welcome party.

"Can I go see if Isabel can play?" I asked.

Abuelita agreed. We went to Isabel's house and rang the doorbell. A few minutes later, Isabel came out with her mom.

"¡Hola, Sandra! Qué gusto verte," Abuelita greeted Isabel's mother. "Nice to see you!"

"Pasen," Isabel's mom said. "Come on in!"

"That's okay. Lola just wanted to see if Isabel could come over to play," Abuelita said.

"Of course," Isabel's mom replied. "I'm glad you stopped by. We are having a party on Friday. You are all invited!"

"¡Muchas gracias!" Abuelita exclaimed. "See you Friday!"

Isabel came with us to Abuelita's house. We played outside in the garden.

I smiled. Isabel didn't seem to think I was acting better than her. Maybe things in Guatemala were looking up after all.

"I wish I could speak Spanish like everyone else," I confessed.

"Let's practice!" Isabel said. "Say something in Spanish!"

"Yo me llamo Lola," I said. "My name is Lola."

"¡Muy bien! You can speak Spanish!" Isabel replied.

"Except for when the words have r's," I said. "I get stuck. My cousin Luis always points it out."

"Say perro, dog" Isabel told me.

"Pe-r-r-o." I stumbled over the r's in the word. "See?"

41

"I have an idea!" Isabel told me. "I'll teach you a tongue twister that I learned when I was little. I think it will help you with your r's!"

I was ready to do anything to make my Spanish better and fit in.

"Tres tristes tigres tragaban trigo en un trigal," Isabel said. "It means, 'Three sad tigers ate wheat at a wheat field.' Think of it as a workout for your tongue!"

I tried to say the tongue twister, but I stumbled over the words.

"Try again," Isabel encouraged me.

We practiced the tongue twister while jumping rope. Every time I got stuck, it was Isabel's turn to jump.

We practiced and practiced. Playing with Isabel reminded me of my friends back home. I missed Joy and Sophia. I imagined how much fun it would be to be all together.

After a while, I was surprised to realize the tongue twister was getting easier!

"You're a great teacher!" I told Isabel. "Listen: tres tristes tigres . . ." The r's rolled off my tongue.

"You did it!" Isabel cheered.

I smiled proudly. What would Luis think if I could say the tongue twister? He would have to be impressed. Isabel's party would be the perfect place to show him.

Chapter 8

The Party

I spent the rest of the week practicing the tongue twister. Finally, Friday night arrived. Luis and his family were invited to the party too. We went to Isabel's house together.

"Don't forget to say hola and give a kiss on the cheek when you meet someone," Abuelita reminded me. "And make sure to smile!"

I nodded. I didn't like saying hi with a kiss. It felt weird and different. But I didn't want to seem rude. I kissed about twenty people—*yuck!* I could not kiss another face!

Thankfully, Isabel rescued me. "Can Lola play?" she asked.

Abuelita nodded. "Remember your manners, Lola. Have fun!" she told me.

"Let's go," Isabel said.

My tummy rumbled loudly.

"I know how to fix that!" said Isabel.

We snuck to the kitchen. Inside, people were preparing food. It looked like a restaurant.

"Let's grab a tray of sweets while we wait for dinner," Isabel said. "But make sure we don't get caught. My mama won't want us ruining our appetites."

We grabbed a fancy silver plate covered with sweets. Then, we snuck out of the kitchen.

Luis saw us and hurried to catch up.

"Where are we going?" he asked.

Isabel pointed down the hall. "To the study!"

We hid in the study with the tray of sweets.

"Lola, say the tongue twister I taught you!" Isabel encouraged me.

I looked at my cousin. I wanted to impress him. Maybe this was my chance.

"Tres tristes tigres, tragaban trigo en un." I paused. "I forgot the last part."

"Trigal," Isabel said.

"Not bad," Luis said. "But I bet you can't do it in front of the whole party."

"Can too," I argued.

"Fine," Luis said. "If you can, I'll tell everyone you're my favorite cousin. But if you mess up, you owe me ten dollars."

"Deal," I said. This was my chance to prove to Luis that I fit in with our family.

"Race you!" Luis said. He grabbed the empty silver tray and ran out of the study.

"I know a shortcut!" Isabel hollered. "Follow me."

I raced after Isabel. But Luis had gone the opposite direction. We crashed into each other coming around a corner.

The empty silver platter flew in the air. It fell to the ground with a loud *BANG!*

I looked around and realized we were in the living room. The entire party stared at us, including Abuelita. And she did *not* look happy.

Chapter 9

Family Is Forever

"Lola, Luis, come with me," Abuelita said. We followed her back to the study.

"Now," Abuelita said once we were alone, "who wants to tell me what is going on with the two of you?"

"I'm sorry, Abuelita!" I said. "Luis—"

"It's Lola's fault!" Luis said at the same time. He pointed at me.

"Enough," Abuelita said. "The only way to solve a problem is to find a solution. Let's figure this out. Lola, you first."

I took a deep breath. "Luis, why don't you like me?" I asked. "Ever since I got here, you've been correcting me! I heard you in the kitchen that first night talking about me."

Luis blushed. "I'm sorry. But you don't live here, and all the attention is always on you. It feels like I'm invisible. And you're always bragging about how great things are back home!"

"I wasn't trying to brag," I said. "I just miss home. And I thought you wanted to learn about me too."

"Why don't we try to find what you have in common instead of pointing out your differences?" Abuelita suggested. "I'll start. You both love the same sport!"

"Soccer!" I cheered.

"¡Fútbol! I didn't know you played!" Luis exclaimed.

"That's my dad's favorite sport," I said. "We play together." I thought for a second. "Do you like onions?" I asked.

"I hate them!" Luis replied.

"Me too!" I giggled.

Abuelita smiled. "What did I tell you? Talking things through is always a good solution," she said. "You two have to be there for each other. Family is forever!"

Abuelita was right. Luis and I had a lot in common. It felt good to talk things through.

"I'm glad you've made up because I have a final surprise for you," Abuelita said. "We are going to spend the weekend at Lake Atitlán!"

"Lake Atitlán!" I cheered. "Dad talks about it all the time."

He loved to tell me about the famous lake. He'd gone to it when he was growing up in Guatemala.

I turned to Luis. "I bet we'll be best friends by the end of the weekend!" I giggled.

Luis grinned. "Or enemies!"

"Luis!" Abuelita exclaimed.

Luis laughed. "Just kidding!"

Chapter 10

Lake Atitlán

I woke up Saturday morning with a smile. *Lake Atitlán, here I come!* I thought.

It was a long drive to the lake, but this time the car ride was fun. Luis and I played games and sang.

Abuelita was right—talking had helped solve our problems.

We finally arrived at the famous lake. I couldn't believe my eyes. Volcanoes and mountains surrounded the lake. The plants were so green that they didn't seem real. It looked like a postcard!

We went to a beautiful restaurant for lunch. Abuelita explained that the chef grew all the food cooked there.

We started with taquitos and tamales. They were delicious!

"Esto es delicioso," I said.

"Your Spanish has improved so much!" Abuelita cheered.

I smiled. "¡Gracias!"

"It was all me!" Luis joked. "Go ahead, show them! Or you can give me my money now. . . ."

I hadn't forgotten about our bet at the party. "Get ready to tell everyone I'm your favorite!" I said.

"Everyone, Lola has something to say!" Luis announced.

"Tres tristes tigres tragaban trigo en un trigal. . ." I said the tongue twister perfectly!

My family gave me a standing ovation.

After lunch, we toured the town of Santiago. We stopped to eat ice cream on the way to the hotel. I saw a beautiful painting for my dad in one of the little shops.

"Abuelo, can I buy that painting for Dad?" I asked.

"Sí, do you need help?" Abuelo replied.

I shook my head. "No, gracias. I've got it!"

Abuelo gave me several colorful bills. This time I was confident with my Spanish.

"¿Qué se le ofrece?" said a man behind the counter.

I smiled. "Buenas tardes," I told him. "Tengo muchos regalos que comprar. I have many presents to buy."

I used my Spanish to buy a painting for Dad and a doll for Mariana. I even got bracelets for my best friends back home. I was so happy!

At the hotel that night, my entire family had fun playing games. I grabbed a soccer ball and turned to Luis.

"¿Jugamos?" I asked.

"¡Vamos!" Luis said. "Let's go!"

We invited all the family to play. I finally felt like I belonged.

"This has been the best trip ever!" I said. "Promise you'll stay in touch when I go back home," I told Luis.

"Definitely," Luis agreed. "Maybe next time I'll come visit you in Texas. I want to see if it is as amazing as you say."

I smiled. My home *was* amazing. But so was Guatemala. I was going to miss it when I left— even Luis.

I couldn't wait to see my parents and little sister. But I had a whole week ahead of me in Guatemala, and I was going to make the most of it!

GLOSSARY

advice (AD-vies)—guidance or recommendation

archaeologist (ar-kee-OL-uh-jist)—a person who learns about the past by digging up old buildings or objects and studying them

heritage (HER-uh-tij)—history and traditions handed down from the past

numeral (NOO-mer-uhl)—a symbol or group of symbols representing a number

opportunity (op-er-TOO-ni-tee)—a chance for greater success

ovation (oh-VEY-shuhn)—an expression of approval or enthusiasm made by clapping or cheering

passport (PASS-port)—an official booklet that proves that a person is a citizen of a certain country; passports allow people to travel to foreign countries

patient (PAY-shunt)—calm during frustrating or difficult times

sculpture (SKUHLP-chur)—something carved or shaped out of rock

university (yoo-nuh-VUR-suh-tee)—a four-year school for higher learning after high school where people can study for degrees

SPANISH GLOSSARY

abuelita (ah-bweh-LEE-tah)—grandmother

abuelo (ah-BWEH-loh)—grandfather

buenas noches (BWEH-nahs NOH-chehs)—good night

buenos días (BWEH-nohs DEE-ahs)—good morning

cafecito (kah-feh-SEE-toh)—a small coffee

canillitas de leche (kah-nee-YEE-tahs deh LEH-cheh)—sweets made with powdered sugar and milk

casa (KAH-sah)—house

estos (EHS-tohs)—these

gracias (GRAH-syahs)—thank you

hola (OH-lah)—hello

perro (PEH-rroh)—dog

¿qué se le ofrece? (keh seh leh oh-FREH-seh)—what do you want?

tengo muchos regalos que comprar (ten-GOH MOO-chohs rreh-GAH-lohs KEH kohm-PRAHR)—I have many gifts/presents to buy

tía (TEE-ah)—aunt

tío (TEE-oh)—uncle

vámonos (VAH-moh-nohs)—let's go

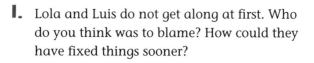

TALK ABOUT IT

1. Lola and Luis do not get along at first. Who do you think was to blame? How could they have fixed things sooner?

2. Lola makes a new friend when she meets Isabel. Have you ever made a new friend? Talk about that person and how you met.

3. Do you know another language? If yes, what is it? How did you learn it? If you don't know another language, what language would you like to learn?

WRITE IT DOWN

1. Imagine that you're in Lola's position and are traveling to a new place for the first time. What would you pack? Make a list of all the important things you'd want to bring.

2. All families argue sometimes. Have you ever had a disagreement with a family member? Write a paragraph about what happened and how you made things work.

3. Luis and Lola agree to try to stay in touch after she goes home to Texas. Follow their lead and write a letter to a friend or family member you have not seen in a while.

ABUELITA'S CHOCOLATE CALIENTE

Lola learns that the secret ingredient in Abuelita's recipe is love. With an adult's help, make chocolate caliente at home—and don't forget the love!

WHAT YOU NEED

- 2 cups milk*
- 4 tablespoons sugar
- 2 tablespoons unsweetened cocoa powder
- salt
- cinnamon
- a medium pot
- a big spoon or a whisk
- 2 mugs to serve

*You can use any type of milk you prefer or use water instead.

WHAT TO DO

1. Pour the milk, sugar, and cocoa powder, into the pot. Add a pinch of salt and a dash of cinnamon.

2. Bring the mixture to a boil and stir until everything is combined and the chocolate is smooth. (Be safe—make sure an adult turns on the stove and supervises while the chocolate is cooking.)

3. Pour the chocolate into mugs. Wait until it cools down a little bit, then enjoy!

Tip: During summer, you can make popsicles with Abuelita's chocolate.

ABOUT THE AUTHOR

Photo credit JCPenney

Keka Novales grew up in Guatemala City, Guatemala, which is located in Central America. Growing up, she wanted to be a doctor, a vet, a ballerina, an engineer, and a writer. Keka moved several times and changed schools, so she has plenty of experience being the "new kid." Her grandparents had a vital role in her life. Abuelo was always making jokes, and Abuelita helped everyone around her. Keka currently lives with her family in Denton, Texas.

ABOUT THE ILLUSTRATOR

Photo credit Gloria Félix

Gloria Félix was born and raised in Uruapan, a beautiful, small city in Michoacán, Mexico. Her home is one of her biggest inspirations when it comes to art. Her favorite things to do growing up were drawing, watching cartoons, and eating, which are still some of her favorite things to do. Gloria currently lives and paints in Los Angeles, California.